SECRET AGENT

Carmel Reilly
Vonda Pestana

Australia • Brazil • Japan • Korea • Mexico • Singapore • Spain • United Kingdom • United States

Secret Agent

Fast Forward
Green Level 14

Text: Carmel Reilly
Illustrations: Vonda Pestana
Editor: Johanna Rohan
Design: Vonda Pestana
Series design: James Lowe
Production controller: Emma Hayes
Audio recordings: Juliet Hill, Picture Start
Spoken by: Matthew King and Abbe Holmes
Reprint: Katherine Fullagar

ISBN 978 0 17 012588 8
ISBN 978 0 17 012585 7 (set)

Cengage Learning Australia
Level 7, 80 Dorcas Street
South Melbourne, Victoria Australia 3205
Phone: 1300 790 853

Cengage Learning New Zealand
Unit 4B Rosedale Office Park
331 Rosedale Road, Albany, North Shore NZ 0632
Phone: 0800 449 725

For learning solutions, visit **cengage.com.au**

Printed in Australia by Ligare Pty Ltd
10 11 12 13 14 15 16 19 18 17 16 15

Evaluated in independent research by staff from the Department of Language, Literacy and Arts Education at the University of Melbourne.

Contents

THE TEST

Trent was running fast. Somewhere behind him was a loud boom!

BOOM

He saw the door and grabbed it.
He pulled it open and dived inside.

Dr Holland was waiting for him.

"Did I pass the test?" asked Trent.

"You did," smiled Dr Holland. "You're now ready to start work as a secret agent."

"Great!" said Trent.

"First, you'll need this,"
said Dr Holland,
handing Trent a bag.
"It's full of agent's things,
like trackers and smoke balls
and …"

Suddenly, there was another blast.
"Is this part of the test, too?"
Trent yelled.
"No!" shouted Dr Holland.
"Get down!"
Trent dived under a bench
and waited.

Then, everything went quiet.
Trent got out and looked around.
The place was a mess.
Dr Holland was gone.

Chapter 2

FOLLOWING THE CAR

Trent knew this had to be the work of enemy agents. Thinking fast, he grabbed the bag and raced outside. He saw two men pushing Dr Holland into a car.

Running Words 154

XYZ
Trent ran towards the car.
As it pulled out into the traffic,
he reached into his bag
and found the tracker.
He threw it hard and it stuck fast
onto the back of the car.

With the tracker stuck on the car,
Trent could follow it.
He ran and got his super skateboard.
A quick look at his watch screen
showed him where the car
was heading.

Seconds later, Trent was swinging his way in and out of the traffic.

Trent found the car parked outside
an old warehouse.
He got off his super skateboard
and crept around the back.
He crept up to a window
and looked in.
The enemy agents were inside
and so was Dr Holland –
tied to a chair.

Chapter 3

TRENT GOES IN

Trent had to act fast.
He found the smoke ball in his bag and threw it in the window.

The smoke hit the enemy agents and they fell to the floor, rubbing their eyes.

Trent put on a mask
and jumped inside.

"Let's get out of here," Trent said.
He rushed over to Dr Holland
and untied her hands.

Trent helped Dr Holland to the door
and tried to open it,
but it was stuck.
He pushed and pulled it,
but no matter what he did,
the door wouldn't open.

A STICKY END

The enemy agents got up
and rushed towards Trent and Dr Holland.
Trent was ready.
He smiled to himself
as he grabbed the roll of
agent's super tape out of his bag.

With a quick flip, he pulled the tape out and threw it towards the enemy agents.

The enemy agents froze
as they looked up at the tape.
But, by the time they started to move,
it was too late.

Trent watched as the tape wrapped around them.

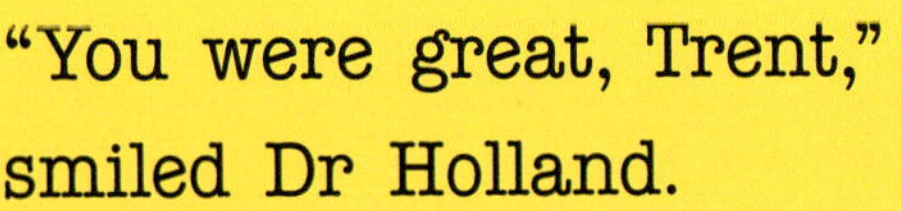

"You were great, Trent," smiled Dr Holland.

"Thanks," said Trent. "That agent's bag really helped. I couldn't have wrapped this up

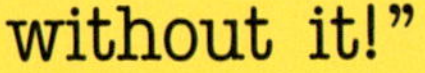

without it!"